SOCCER SPIRIT

BY JAKE MADDOX

illustrated by Tuesday Mourning

text by Eric Stevens

Librarian Reviewer
Chris Kreie
Media Specialist, Eden Prairie Schools, MN
MS in Information Media, St. Cloud State University, MN

Reading Consultant
Mary Evenson
Middle School Teacher, Edina Public Schools, MN
MA in Education, University of Minnesota

Impact Books are published by Stone Arch Books
151 Good Counsel Drive, P.O. Box 669
Mankato, Minnesota 56002
www.stonearchbooks.com

Library of Congress Cataloging-in-Publication Data
Maddox, Jake.
    Soccer Spirit / Jake Maddox; illustrated by Tuesday Mourning.
    p. cm. — (Impact Books. A Jake Maddox Sports Story)
    ISBN 978-1-4342-0780-7 (library binding)
    ISBN 978-1-4342-0876-7 (pbk.)
    [1. Soccer—Fiction. 2. Teamwork (Sports)—Fiction.] I. Mourning,
Tuesday, ill. II. Title.
PZ7.M25643Soc 2009
[Fic]—dc22   2008004296

Summary: When the girls' soccer team is canceled, three girls have to
join their arch rival team.

Art Director: Heather Kindseth
Graphic Designer: Kay Fraser

1 2 3 4 5 6 13 12 11 10 09 08

Printed in the United States of America

TABLE OF CONTENTS

* CHAPTER 1 *

BAD NEWS

Anna Reed crouched slightly in the goal and squinted up the field. She smiled as she watched Brittany West kick the soccer ball down the empty field they used for practice. Brittany was a great ball handler. She was also Anna's best friend.

"You can't stop me!" Brittany yelled as she moved closer to the goal.

Anna watched Brittany's feet carefully. She stayed ready to pounce.

Brittany was tricky. She'd make goalies think she was shooting low. Then she would go high with her shot. She was also good at faking left, then shooting right.

Brittany planted her left foot and got ready to shoot. Anna bent down and bounced slightly, ready to block. It looked like Brittany was shooting right.

Then Brittany kicked. Just at the last second, Anna realized the shot was going left. She leaped across the goal. Just before the ball flew into the net, Anna was able to tap it with her left hand. It went off course and missed the net.

Anna hit the ground hard, but she was smiling. She stood up and brushed the dirt off her T-shirt and shorts.

"Nice shot, Brittany," Anna said to her friend. "But not nice enough."

"How'd you know I was going left?" Brittany asked. "I was sure you'd think I was going right."

Anna shrugged. "Just psychic, I guess," she said, smiling. "Anyway, that was a great shot. East Side doesn't stand a chance this year!" East Side Middle School was their school's biggest rival in girls' soccer.

"Especially with you in goal!" Brittany replied.

Anna sighed. "Looks like it's getting late," she said. "I better get home."

Brittany nodded. "Yeah," she said. "Dinner's probably waiting for me, too."

"See you tomorrow," Anna said.

Brittany rolled her eyes. "First day of school," she said. "Oh joy."

Anna waved. Then she jogged home.

"Dad!" Anna called as she walked into her apartment. "I'm home!"

She walked into the TV room. Her dad put down his newspaper. "There's mail for you," he said. "From school."

"From school?" Anna said, worried. Mail from school was usually bad news, but she hadn't even started classes yet.

"Have a seat," Dad said.

He picked up a letter from the coffee table in front of him. After a quick glance at it, he handed it to Anna.

"Who is it from?" Anna asked.

"Well, read it!" Dad replied.

Anna read the letter. It was from Coach Zimmerman, the girls' soccer coach.

"What?" Anna yelled as she reached the last line. "I can't believe this!"

"I know," Dad replied. "I can understand why you'd be upset."

"I have to call Brittany!" Anna replied.

Dad nodded. "Okay," he said. "Try to be quick, though. Dinner is ready."

Anna ran to her bedroom and quickly dialed Brittany's house. "Did you hear?" Anna practically yelled into the phone.

"Hear what?" Brittany replied.

"Didn't you get a letter from school today?" Anna said. "About funding for athletics?"

"Yes, I did," Brittany said. "What are we going to do? No funding means no girls' soccer team this year!"

CHAPTER 2

COMBINED?

"This is the worst news ever," Jasmine Alito said the next day at lunch. She stared down at her green beans. Jasmine was the best defender on the Lincoln Middle School girls' soccer team, the Eagles.

Even though Jasmine was much taller than Anna and Brittany, she was like a little sister to them. They were all in eighth grade, but Jasmine had skipped a grade and was a year younger.

"Jasmine's right!" Anna said. "How are we going to survive school without the soccer team?" she asked.

"There's Coach Zimmerman!" Jasmine said. She jumped up and walked over to the coach. Anna and Brittany followed her.

"Coach!" Anna called.

"Hi, girls," the coach replied. She looked worried and upset.

"Coach Z, tell us what's going on!" Jasmine said. "No girls' soccer team this year?"

Coach Zimmerman frowned. "I'm afraid that's right, Jasmine," she replied. "We just couldn't afford to have a girls' soccer team at Lincoln this year."

"But there's going to be a boys' team!" Anna pointed out. "That's not fair!"

Coach Zimmerman shook her head. "I know," she said, "but some players from East Side are joining because their funds were cut as well. The girls' team would have only had you three, plus Diana and Eve. That's not even enough for a starting lineup. We probably would have had to cancel the team anyway, even without the funding cut. All the schools in the county are being affected."

"But we want to play!" Anna said.

"Yeah!" Brittany added.

Coach Zimmerman sighed. "I know. I think we've figured something out," she replied. "I'm on my way to meet with Principal Jackson right now about an idea that might work." The coach patted Anna on the shoulder and tried to smile. Then she walked off toward the principal's office.

As Anna, Brittany, and Jasmine sat in class an hour later, Principal Jackson's voice crackled over the PA system.

"Attention, attention," the principal's voice said. "Any girls who wish to play soccer this season should meet with Coach Zimmerman immediately after school today."

The principal continued, "Due to a lack of funds for soccer at our school and East Side Middle School, the teams have been combined."

"What?" half the class said at once.

"No way," Jasmine said.

Anna's mouth hung open. "We have to play with East Side," she said. "Our biggest rivals!"

★ CHAPTER 3 ★

ENEMIES

Anna, Brittany, and Jasmine sat by the window in their last class of the day. Anna stared out the window at the soccer field.

It's not much of a field, she thought. The grass was mostly brown or gone completely. Even from where she was sitting, she could see rocky patches on the field. And the goals were bent and their nets were torn and falling off in places.

"Anna," Brittany said. "Wake up."

"Huh?" Anna replied, turning away from the window. "Is it time to go?"

Brittany shook her head. "No," she replied, "but you were daydreaming. We have to finish this assignment."

"I know," Anna said. "Just thinking about soccer. I'll miss playing on our field."

"That old, nasty field?" Brittany said, nodding toward the window. "You're crazy."

Anna shrugged. "Whatever," she said.

"I'm excited about playing at East Side," Brittany went on in a whisper. "Remember how nice their field is?"

"Of course," Anna said, thinking about their rival's perfect athletics field.

Jasmine turned around in her seat. "Talking about the soccer team?" she asked.

Anna and Brittany nodded. Brittany was smiling, but Anna seemed a little down.

"Are you worried, Anna?" Jasmine asked. "Me too."

"What are you worried about?" Brittany asked.

"Are you kidding?" Jasmine replied. "It's East Side Middle School! Our enemies! What if their players don't even want us around?"

Anna opened her eyes wide. "Whoa," she said. "I hadn't even thought of that."

Suddenly, Brittany wasn't smiling either.

After the bell rang, the girls grabbed their bags and darted from class. Mr. Conrad barely had time to call after them, "Don't forget! Page ten in your textbook, for tomorrow!"

"Ugh," Brittany said as she jogged toward Coach Zimmerman's office. "Homework already."

The coach was waiting for them in her office, along with Diana and Eve.

"Hi, Di," Anna said with a wave. "Hi, Eve."

The other girls smiled and said hello. Then Coach Zimmerman clapped her hands. "Okay, girls," she said. "Let's get to the bus."

"Take a deep breath, everybody," Brittany said. "We're going where no Eagle has gone before."

CHAPTER 4

ALWAYS BE EAGLES

The yellow bus pulled up in front of East Side Middle School. All of the girls stared out the windows.

East Side Middle School was huge, and it looked brand new. It was all cement and big windows. It was set on a big green field of grass. Green hills rose up behind it.

"Here we are," Coach Zimmerman said as the driver opened the door. "Everyone out."

The girls got off the bus and stood around their coach. "All right, Eagles," Coach Zimmerman said. "We're guests here at East Side, so be good."

The girls all nodded.

"And one more thing," the coach added as they started walking toward the entrance. "You'll be called Tigers now, but you'll always be Eagles to me. Got it?"

The girls all smiled. They followed Coach Zimmerman through the school toward the big courtyard, where the soccer field was. The coach pushed open the big metal doors and the five Eagles stepped outside.

The East Side Middle School soccer field was bright green. The boundaries and center line were all freshly painted. The goals looked brand new.

All around the field were stands for students, teachers, and families to watch games. Girls' soccer was very important at East Side Middle School.

"Soccer is way more important here than at Lincoln," Anna mumbled to herself.

"What?" Brittany whispered.

Anna shook her head. "Nothing," she replied. Then she nodded toward the field. "Check it out."

The Tigers were all gathered on the field. There were about fifteen of them, and they were all wearing the Tigers uniform.

"They look like a commercial," Brittany whispered.

The uniforms were bright yellow, with red and white numbers and red and white stripes on the sleeves and shorts.

One person among the Tigers was wearing a red warm-up jacket and pants. She was about the same height as the players, but her hair was very short and bright white. "That must be their coach," Jasmine said.

Eve nodded. "Yup," she said. "I hear she's pretty tough."

"Coach Zimmerman?" the coach called. She waved. "Come on over!"

The girls followed Coach Zimmerman toward the middle of the field. The East Side girls watched as the Lincoln girls walked up. Anna thought that the East Side players didn't seem happy to have guests.

"Hi," Coach Zimmerman said as she shook the other coach's hand. "Call me Coach Z."

"All right, Coach Z," said the other coach. "I'm Coach Suzy."

Brittany leaned over to Eve. "Coach Suzy?" she whispered. "Sounds tough."

The other girls giggled. Coach Zimmerman shot them a look and they quieted down.

"Well, Coach Suzy," Coach Zimmerman said, "here are your new players from Lincoln Middle School."

Coach Suzy turned to the Lincoln girls and wrinkled her brow. "Hmm," she said. "Looks like a good bunch."

Then Coach Suzy squinted at Anna. "Aren't you Anna Reed?" she said. "And you're Brittany West, right?"

Anna and Brittany looked at each other. "Yup," they replied together.

A couple of girls from the East Side team stepped forward. They looked at Anna and Brittany.

Coach Suzy smiled at Anna and Brittany. "I remember you two from last year," she said. "For some reason, I thought you were in eighth grade last year, from how well you played. But now I remember that you were in seventh."

The two girls from East Side who had moved to the front looked at each other. Then they whispered something.

"Right," Anna said. "We're in eighth."

"Great," Coach Suzy said. "The Tigers will be lucky to have you."

"Right," said the taller of the two whispering East Side girls. "Very lucky." She glared at Anna.

★ CHAPTER 5 ★

LUCK

"Okay," Coach Suzy said. She blew her whistle. "Let's get started with tryouts!"

The East Side girls all ran to one end of the field. "Okay," Jasmine said. "I guess we should go with them." The five Lincoln girls ran after the others.

"Everyone line up," Coach Suzy called. "We're going to do some dribbling drills, some passing drills, some shooting drills, and then a scrimmage."

Anna glanced at one of the girls who had been whispering. The girl was pretty tall, and had long blond hair. Her jersey said the name "Rivers."

"That's Lindsay Rivers," said Diana in her ear. "She's the goalie. She started last year, too, just like you."

Anna nodded. "Cool," she said.

"And with her, that's Marissa Lee," Diana added. Marissa was short and had straight black hair. "She's a defender. Not great, but she did start last year."

"Think she'll be competition for Jasmine?" Anna asked.

Diana bit her lip. "Hm," she said. "Maybe. Jasmine is better, if you ask me, and really tough. But maybe Coach Suzy will treat her own players better."

Anna nodded. "Yeah," she said.

The drills went on for almost an hour. Then the scrimmage started.

"Anna," Coach Suzy called out once the girls had gathered around. "You're goalie for team A. Lindsay, you're on team B."

Lindsay glared at Anna with a smirk and mouthed at her, "You're going down."

"Bring it," Anna mouthed back.

"Yeah!" Brittany called to Lindsay. "Bring it!"

"Okay, enough of that," Coach Suzy said with a little chuckle. "Team A, throw on some blue jerseys, and let's get going."

All the Lincoln girls were placed on team A. Anna was relieved. She knew how her old teammates played, and what to expect.

Brittany took a pass off the kickoff and headed down field. Anna smiled.

"Think she'll score on Lindsay?" Jasmine said from her position near the crease.

"No doubt!" Anna called back. "She was the best scorer in the league!"

The girls watched as Brittany faked out two defenders, including Marissa. "Here comes the shot," Anna said. "Watch. She's going high in the right corner."

Anna was right, but Lindsay didn't expect it. She dove high to the left.

"Goal!" Jasmine called, running up to midfield to give Brittany a hug. "Nice one!"

"Celebrate later, please," Coach Suzy said over team A's cheering. Then she grabbed the ball and dropped it in the middle for the kickoff.

Lindsay wasn't fooled again by Brittany, or anyone else. But Anna didn't let in even one goal, so Lindsay's one mistake lost the game. Team A won 1–0.

While Jasmine, Brittany, and Anna were talking after the game, Lindsay and Marissa walked over to them.

"Lucky shot, Brittany," Lindsay said. "It won't happen again."

"Lucky?" Brittany said, looking Lindsay up and down. "That was not luck."

Marissa rolled her eyes. Then she and Lindsay walked off.

"Nice game to you too," Anna mumbled as the two other girls walked away.

"Don't worry about her," another East Side girl said. She was about Anna's height, and had curly dark hair.

"She's just worried because she's actually got some competition in goal this year," the girl went on. "I'm Kaitlyn, by the way."

"Hi, Kaitlyn," Anna said. "I'm Anna, and this is Jasmine and Brittany. And that's Diana and Eve over there."

Kaitlyn nodded. "I know who you guys are," she said. "I wasn't on the team last year, but I went to the games. I saw you two play a few times. You're really great."

"Thanks," Brittany said. "You were pretty good out there today too."

"I hope so," Kaitlyn said. "It'll be fun playing offense with you if I make the starting lineup."

Suddenly Coach Suzy blew two sharp blasts on her whistle. All the girls gathered around her.

"Nice job, team A," Coach Suzy said. "I was really impressed with everyone today. And I'll post the lineup by Thursday afternoon." She smiled.

"Lincoln girls," she went on, "Coach Z will post the results at your school then too. Now hit the showers!"

The sun started to set as the Lincoln bus bounced along toward their school. "Boy, Lindsay Rivers is not my favorite person," Brittany said.

"Don't let her get to you," Anna said. "Besides, I'm the one who's competing with her for starting goalie."

"You'll get it for sure, Anna," Jasmine said.

"No doubt," Brittany added. "The three of us are definitely starting. I promise."

★ CHAPTER 6 ★

THE LINEUP

The next few days were tough. Even though Anna, Brittany, and Jasmine were confident, they didn't know for sure they would make the team. And they really didn't know if they'd get to be on the starting lineup.

"It's just not fair," Brittany said. She was pacing in front of the bulletin board near the locker room. They were waiting for Coach Zimmerman to post the list.

"I mean, if we had a Lincoln team this year," Brittany went on, "we'd all be starters . . . easy!"

The others watched Brittany walk back and forth. "You said that already," Jasmine said. "And you're making me nervous with all your walking back and forth, and back and forth and back and forth."

"Nervous?" Anna joked. "You're making me dizzy!"

Everyone laughed, except for Brittany.

"How could you be anything but nervous?" Brittany said. "Or sick? I'm both!"

"Try to relax," Anna said. "Coach Z will be here with the list any second."

"I can't relax," Brittany said. "I have to keep moving."

"Hi, girls," Coach Z said suddenly. "I think I have what you're waiting for!"

"How does it look?" Brittany asked. She leaned over Coach Z's shoulder as she put up the list. The other girls jumped up and ran over to the board.

"I think you'll all be pretty pleased," Coach Zimmerman said. She smiled and stood back.

"We all made it!" Jasmine said.

"Yes!" Diana said.

"And you're starting on defense, Jasmine," Eve pointed out.

"And I'm starting center!" Brittany shouted.

"I'm not surprised," Jasmine said, giving Brittany a hug.

"What about me?" Anna said, trying to get a look at the list from behind her friends.

"Of course you made it," Brittany said. "And . . . oh."

"Oh?" Anna said, finally checking out the list. "What do you mean, oh?"

Anna looked down the list of names. She had made the team, all right. But there it was, in black and white: "Starting goalie: Lindsay Rivers."

⋆ CHAPTER 7 ⋆

UNFAIR

"I can't believe this," Jasmine said. The Lincoln girls were sitting on their bus on the way to East Side for practice. "It's totally unfair!"

"Unfair?" Brittany said. She bounced out of her seat as the bus hit a bump. "It's more than unfair!"

Eve shook her head. "I thought for sure Anna would start after Lindsay let in that goal of yours, Brittany," she said.

Brittany gritted her teeth. "Aren't you angry, Anna?" she asked.

Anna shrugged. She was disappointed, but she didn't want to let herself get angry. "I guess I'm a little angry," she finally said.

"Coach Z!" Brittany called to the front of the bus. "Can you do anything about this?"

Coach Zimmerman smiled weakly and shook her head. "Sorry, girls," she said. "I'm disappointed too, but I'm not the coach anymore. There's nothing I can do."

"You're still our coach," Jasmine said. "I mean, like you said, we're still Eagles, right?"

Coach Zimmerman nodded. "Sure, and I'm still the Eagles' coach. But when it comes to the Tigers, I don't have any power at all."

"None?" Anna said. "We all thought you were, like, the second coach!"

Coach Zimmerman laughed lightly. "Nope," she said. "I'll be coming to as many practices with you girls as I can, because I care about you and love to watch you play and win! But you're Tigers this year, which means you're Coach Suzy's team. And she's the only coach you have."

Anna slumped in her seat.

When the Lincoln girls arrived at the courtyard soccer field, the East Side girls were in uniform and waiting. Lindsay and Marissa ran over to Anna right away.

"So, Second String," Lindsay said to Anna with a sneer, "decided to show up?"

"Of course I showed up," Anna said. "I'm on the team. Why wouldn't I?"

Marissa laughed and Lindsay shushed her with a wicked smile.

"Oh, I don't know," Lindsay said, looking back at Anna. "I'm not sure I'd show up if I were you."

"Watch it, Lindsay," Brittany said, stepping up. Lindsay glared at her.

"Just leave me alone, Lindsay, okay?" Anna replied. She turned away and started to do some stretches, trying to look like Lindsay's comments hadn't bothered her.

The truth was, though, they had.

* CHAPTER 8 *

SECOND STRING

The Tigers' first game came quickly. After a week of practices, Anna and her friends were starting to feel at home.

Lindsay and her sidekick, Marissa, had even let up the teasing a little. Still, Anna sometimes caught the two East Side girls whispering and looking at her.

Before the first game was about to start, Anna sat on the Tigers' bench.

Kaitlyn was kicking the ball around in front of the goal. She spotted Anna on the bench. "Hi," Kaitlyn said as she sat down next to Anna.

"Hi, Kaitlyn," Anna replied. "Nice shot. It was a really good one."

"Thanks," said Kaitlyn. "I've seen Lindsay play so many times, I know all her problems. She's easy for me to score on."

"Are you starting today?" Anna asked.

"Yup," Kaitlyn said. "Right wing."

Anna nodded. She watched Jasmine and Brittany pass the ball, while Di and Eve tried to stop them.

"Don't worry about it, Anna," Kaitlyn said. "I'm sure Coach Suzy will let you play today. She just knows Lindsay so well. She's seen her play so many times."

"I guess," Anna said, looking at her feet. She tried to smile. When she looked up at the field again, Lindsay and Marissa were standing in their goal, whispering and watching her.

"Don't even pay attention to Lindsay," Kaitlyn said. "She just knows she's got competition now."

Anna shrugged. "If you say so," she said.

"Trust me, you'll be playing before the end of the game," Kaitlyn said.

Once the game had started, Anna started to feel better. She loved watching soccer almost as much as she loved playing it.

Kaitlyn and Brittany each scored one goal. After Anna had watched Lindsay make some very nice saves, she had to admit that Lindsay was pretty great at goal.

With only a couple of minutes left, Coach Suzy put her hand on Anna's shoulder. "Okay, Anna," the coach said. "Let's see what you've got."

Anna looked up. "You want me in? Now?" Anna asked.

Coach Suzy nodded. "Yup," she said. Then she called, "Lindsay, take a seat."

Lindsay looked over at the sidelines and shot the coach a confused look. Coach Suzy waved her over, and she shrugged and jogged toward the bench.

Anna got to her feet. Smiling, she took over at goal. She passed Lindsay on the way. "Good luck, Second String," Lindsay said with a sneer.

Anna ignored her and took her place in front of the goal.

Okay, she thought. *Here we go. Time to show these Tigers what you're made of.*

She didn't have to wait long. The other team's center was driving with both wings, and a shot would be coming soon.

The center faked out Marissa. Then the center passed around Jasmine to the right wing.

"Here she comes," Anna said to herself. She was ready to spring at the shot.

Then it came. Anna watched the girl's feet closely. She pulled back, looking left and low, but Anna saw her foot turning. The girl was definitely shooting to the right. There was no doubt about it.

Anna dove to her right just as the shot took off. The ball hit her in the stomach, and she hugged it against her.

Blocked!

"Woo!" Brittany called from midfield. "Nice save, Reed!"

Anna didn't take the time to celebrate. She immediately got to her feet, held the ball in both hands, and drew back to kick.

Anna's kick was long and high. By the time it hit the ground, the game was over.

"Great save, Anna," Coach Suzy said when the players returned to the bench after the final whistle.

"Thanks, Coach Suzy," Anna replied, smiling.

She grabbed a towel from the bench and wiped her face. When she pulled the towel away, Coach Suzy had walked off.

Lindsay and Marissa were standing there. They glared at Anna.

"It didn't even matter," Marissa told Anna. "We would have won even if they scored."

"Yeah," added Lindsay. "Besides, it was just a lucky leap . . . Second String."

* CHAPTER 9 *

IMPOSSIBLE

The next game was a few days later. Before the game, Coach Suzy walked back and forth with her clipboard. All the Tigers sat on the bench.

"You girls have been looking great in practice," Coach Suzy said. "Today we're going to try a few new things."

The coach listed a few new positions and switched some players around. Kaitlyn was getting a shot at center.

"Nice job, Kaitlyn," Brittany said. "You'll do great."

"Thanks," Kaitlyn replied.

"And starting in goal," Coach Suzy went on, "let's see Anna today."

Lindsay jumped up. "What?" she yelled. "After my perfect game the other day?"

"Take a seat, please, Lindsay," Coach Suzy said without looking up. "Let's not compete with our teammates, okay?"

Lindsay sat back on the bench. "This is totally unfair," she mumbled to herself. Marissa sat down next to her and glared at Anna.

"Don't let them bug you," Kaitlyn said. "Just play your best."

Coach Suzy blew her whistle. "All right," she said. "Let's do this!"

The game was very close. After thirty minutes, the score was still 0–0. Anna had blocked a few shots, and Brittany and Kaitlyn had each been stopped by the other team's goalie a couple of times. Something big would have to happen soon.

Kaitlyn tried a side pass to Brittany, but the other team got it. Soon the other team was driving down the field. Jasmine tried to cut them off, but the other team's wing made a great pass clear across the field.

"Keep it away!" Anna called up to her defense. Marissa looked back at Anna and smirked.

What's she smiling about? Anna wondered.

Then, just as the other team's offense was about to corner themselves out of shot range, Marissa tumbled.

"Whoa!" Marissa cried as she hit the ground.

The other team's offense suddenly had nothing between them and Anna's goal. All three players charged her. Jasmine couldn't get over to cover Marissa's position in time. It would all be up to Anna.

The center pulled back to shoot, but as Anna watched her feet, she knew she would pass instead. Now the wing had the ball, and she was moving in fast on the right. Anna turned to face her, expecting a shot, but the wing passed across the crease.

Anna jumped to her left, but they were too fast for her. The other wing pulled back and shot behind Anna. She tried to change directions, but in midair, it was impossible.

"Goal!" the referee called out.

CHAPTER 10

JUST SLIPPED?

Anna got to her feet and brushed off her jersey and shorts. Marissa was standing at the top of the crease, smiling at her.

"Way to go, Second String," Marissa said. "Way to lose the game for us."

"Her?" Brittany yelled as she stormed downfield. "You're blaming her for losing the game for us? What did you do, Marissa? Slip on a banana peel or something?"

Marissa smiled nervously and looked around. "What . . . what are you talking about?" she asked.

"We all saw you take a dive," Jasmine said. "Was it just to make Anna look dumb?"

"I did not take a dive," Marissa said. "I just slipped."

Anna looked over at the bench. Lindsay was hanging her head and Coach Suzy was heading toward Marissa, Brittany, and Jasmine on the field.

A moment later, Diana was taking Marissa's place on defense.

"Anna, don't worry about that goal," Diana said. "Coach Suzy is angry at Marissa. Even Lindsay seems angry at her."

"Really?" Anna asked. "Even Lindsay?"

Diana nodded as play started at midfield. "Yup," she said, jogging away to join the game in action. "Lindsay said something about not wanting to lose a game just so she could start again."

Anna was shocked. Could it be that Lindsay cared enough about her team to give Anna a fair chance?

Brittany was fired up after Marissa's fall. She immediately drove for the other goal and made a great shot around one defender, fooling their goalie completely. The score was 1–1. A few minutes later, Jasmine got a pass and kicked the ball up to Kaitlyn. Kaitlyn scored, making the score 2–1, East Side.

There were only a few seconds left. "We got this!" Anna shouted, clapping.

But the other team wasn't ready to lose yet. Their offense started driving up the field. Their center faked around Jasmine and passed it off to their right wing. Diana tried to steal the ball, but the other team's right wing passed it right between her legs!

Uh-oh, Anna thought. *They want to tie this game really badly.*

Anna crouched and watched the offense approach. "Here we go again," she mumbled. She was facing their offense alone, for the second time in one game.

The center passed it off to the wing, just like last time. Anna stayed ready. The wing passed it fast and hard across the crease to the other wing, just like last time.

This time, Anna didn't jump too soon. She watched the wing's feet.

At the exact right moment, as the ball went high and to the right, Anna bounced. She knocked the ball with the tip of her fingers and made the save.

"Yes!" she cried, as she hit the ground.

"Nice save, Anna!" Brittany called.

"We won!" Jasmine added, pumping her fist.

Anna got to her feet and dusted herself off. The students and parents in the stands went crazy cheering for her great save.

"Nice save, Second String," Lindsay said as the whole team gathered in the crease to celebrate. "I mean, Anna. Nice save."

Anna smiled at her. "Thanks, Lindsay," she said. "Hope you won't mind sharing this goal with me for the rest of the season."

"I'll be happy to," Lindsay said. "And I'm sorry." She raised her hand for Anna to slap.

"Don't worry about it," Anna said, slapping Lindsay's hand and smiling. "After all, we're both Tigers, right?"

ABOUT THE AUTHOR

Eric Stevens lives in St. Paul, Minnesota. He is studying to become a middle-school English teacher. Some of his favorite things include pizza, playing video games, watching cooking shows on TV, riding his bike, and trying new restaurants. Some of his least favorite things include olives and shoveling snow.

ABOUT THE ILLUSTRATOR

When Tuesday Mourning was a little girl, she knew she wanted to be an artist when she grew up. Now, she is an illustrator who lives in Knoxville, Tennessee. She especially loves illustrating books for kids and teenagers. When she isn't illustrating, Tuesday loves spending time with her husband, who is an actor, and their son, Atticus.

GLOSSARY

athletics (ath-LET-iks)—competitive sports

competition (kom-puh-TISH-uhn)—if someone or something is your competition, you are competing with them, or you are both trying to get the same thing

enemies (EN-uh-meez)—those you are fighting against

funding (FUHN-ding)—money for something

immediately (i-MEE-dee-it-lee)—right away

psychic (SYE-kik)—someone who can tell what will happen in the future

rival (RYE-vuhl)—someone whom you are competing against

second string (SEK-uhnd STRING)—if you are second string, you are not number one

sidekick (SYDE-kik)—someone's close friend or partner

SOCCER WORDS

boundaries (BOUN-duh-reez)—the lines on the edge of the soccer field

center (SEN-tur)—one of the players whose goal is to score points

center line (SEN-tur LINE)—the line that divides the soccer field in half

crease (CREES)—the area near the goal

defender (di-FEN-dur)—a person playing defense, trying to keep the other team from scoring

drills (DRILZ)—a way to practice something, by doing it over and over

goalie (GOL-ee)—the person whose role is to stop the other team from scoring by blocking their shots

kickoff (KIK-off)—at the beginning of the game, the kickoff decides which team has control of the ball

YOU SHOULD KNOW

lineup (LINE-uhp)—the list of which person will be playing which position

midfield (MID-feeld)—the middle part of the field

offense (AW-fenss)—the team that is attacking or trying to score, or the players whose jobs it is to score

referee (REF-uh-REE)—someone who supervises a sports match and makes sure that all the players follow the rules

scrimmage (SKRIM-ij)—a game played for practice, usually between members of the same team

starting (STAR-ting)—if someone is a starting player, they are one of the players who are first on the field

wing (WING)—an attacking player

DISCUSSION QUESTIONS

1. At Lincoln, the only option for girls' soccer was to join the East Side soccer team. Can you think of other ways that the girls in this book could have played soccer, without having to join another school's team?

2. If you had to choose between joining another school's team or quitting your favorite sport, which would you pick? Explain your answer.

3. How do you think the girls at East Side Middle School felt to have new girls joining their team?

WRITING PROMPTS

1. Have you ever had to cooperate with someone from a rival team or group? How did you make it work? What happened? Write about it.

2. Has anyone ever been mean to you on a sports team or in another group? Write about what happened.

3. At the end of this book, Anna and Lindsay are nice to each other. What do you think happens next? Write a page that tells what happens the next time that Anna and Lindsay see each other.

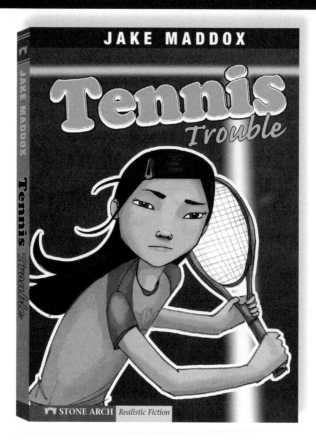

Alexis made the varsity tennis team. She's
thrilled, but some older girls are out to make
Alexis's season terrible. Can she keep up her
self-confidence and step up to the net, or will
she let the girls get to her and lose everything?

BY JAKE MADDOX

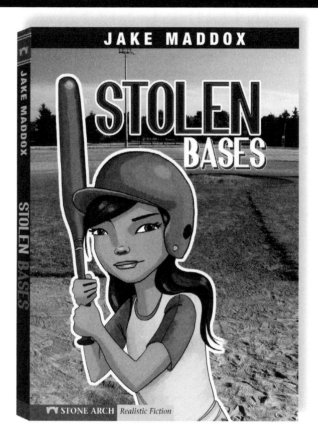

One day at softball practice, the bag of
equipment is gone. The next day, it's been
returned. When the bag disappears again, Eva
and Becca decide to try to catch the crook. But
the person they find is not who they expect!

INTERNET SITES
IS 61 LIBRARY

Do you want to know more about subjects related to this book? Or are you interested in learning about other topics? Then check out FactHound, a fun, easy way to find Internet sites.

Our investigative staff has already sniffed out great sites for you!

Here's how to use FactHound:

1. Visit *www.facthound.com*

2. Select your grade level.

3. To learn more about subjects related to this book, type in the book's ISBN number: **9781434207807**.

4. Click the **Fetch It** button.

FactHound will fetch the best Internet sites for you!